KACHINAS

COLOR AND CUT-OUT COLLECTION

Kachina dolls represent the mysterious and powerful spirit beings of the Hopi. These spirits live in the sky, the springs and the high mountain peaks of Arizona. The dolls are made by dancers dressed as kachinas and are presented to children. The children take the dolls home, where they serve as important reminders of the beauty, deep meaning and beneficial strength of the kachinas.

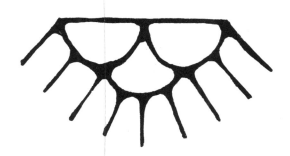

ADAPTED FROM HOPI ORIGINALS

BY

JULIE WEST STAHELI

 TROUBADOR PRESS
a subsidiary of
PRICE STERN SLOAN

GENERAL INSTRUCTIONS

The dolls are constructed by forming each body part into a cylinder, secured by alphabetically labeled tabs and slits.

1. **Color the doll.** The traditional colors are described on the *reverse* side of each figure.
2. **Using scissors or mat knife, cut the doll out along heavy outside lines; cut along dotted lines in interior of figure.**
3. **Assemble doll by inserting folded tabs into correspondingly lettered slits, then unfolding tab ends inside cylinders, as shown here:**

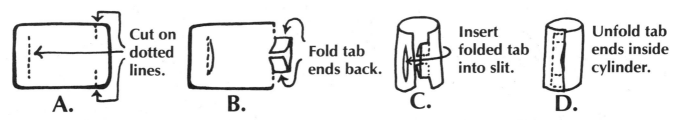

4. **After securing leg cylinders, fold feet up:**

5. **For more graceful posture, arms may be gently folded as follows:***

    ***except: KWA (fold at shoulders only)**

        HEMIS MANA
        TSITOTO   **(fold at wrists and elbows only)**
        TUMAS

6. **Be sure to note and complete any special instructions on individual dolls.**
7. **Each doll will stand alone. For prolonged display, however, place a small circle of masking tape (sticky side out) under one foot.**

MATERIALS NEEDED:

1. **Paints, crayons or markers**
2. **Scissors, mat knife or razor blade**
3. **Tape and glue**

ISBN: 0-8431-1722-2

10 9 8 7 6 5 4 3

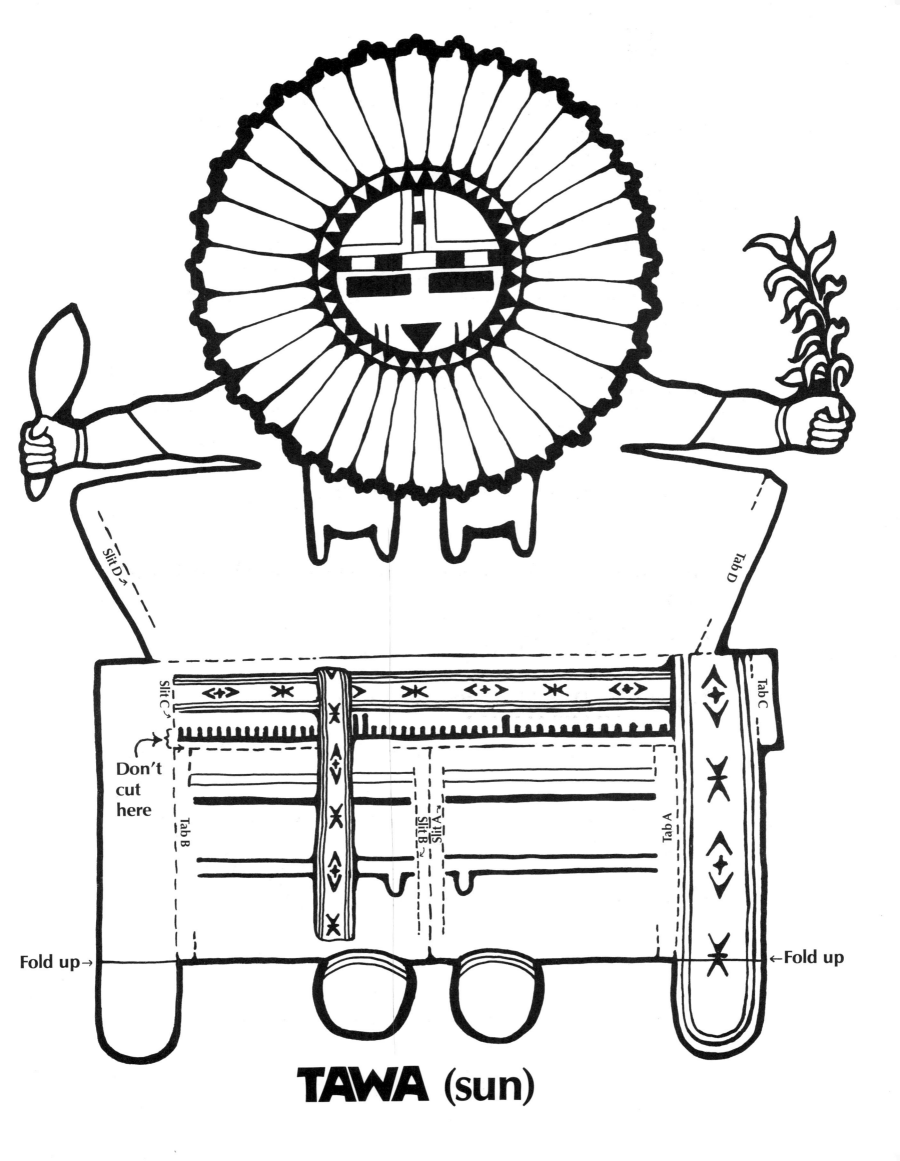

TAWA (sun)

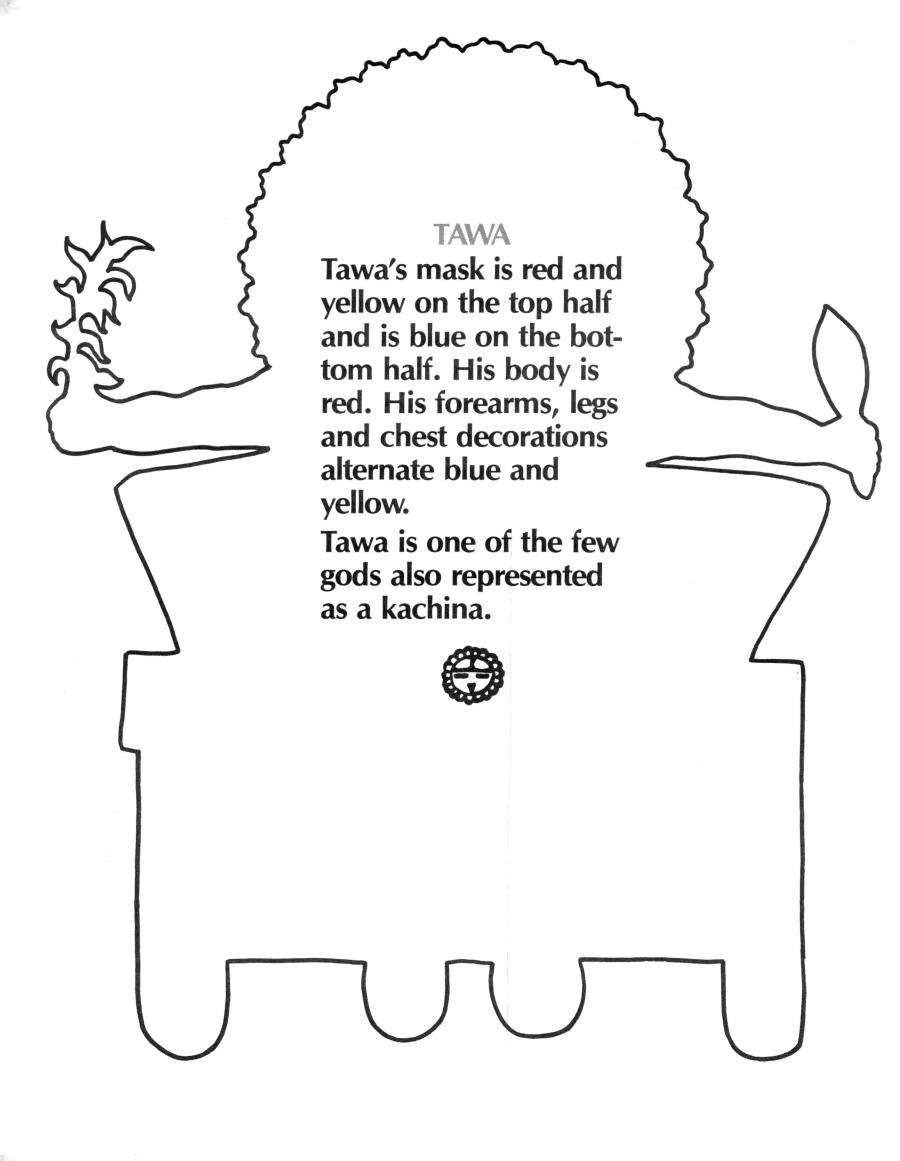

TAWA

Tawa's mask is red and yellow on the top half and is blue on the bottom half. His body is red. His forearms, legs and chest decorations alternate blue and yellow.

Tawa is one of the few gods also represented as a kachina.

Cut out
extra feathers
and insert into
slits on forehead

Slit C

Tab C

extra
feather

fold
here

Close tabs
insert
open tabs

fold
here

extra
feather

Tab B

Slit B

Slit A

Tab A

POLIK MANA (butterfly maid)

POLIK MANA

Polik Mana's head-dress is red, white and yellow.

Her mask is white with blue, red and yellow.

Her dress is black with green and red stripes and her ankle bracelets are red with patterns in blue, green and white.

She grinds corn in a symbolic ritual.

Cut beak on bottom, fold up, turn tip down

Slit F

Tab F

Slit E

Tab E

Tab B

Slit B

Slit A

Tab A

Tab D

Slit D

Slit C

Tab C

MONGWA

(owl)

MONGWA

Mongwa's face and body are white; the rabbit pelt he wears is gray. His sash is green, black, blue, red and white.

During the ceremonies, he spies on the clowns. In times of war, he aids warriors.

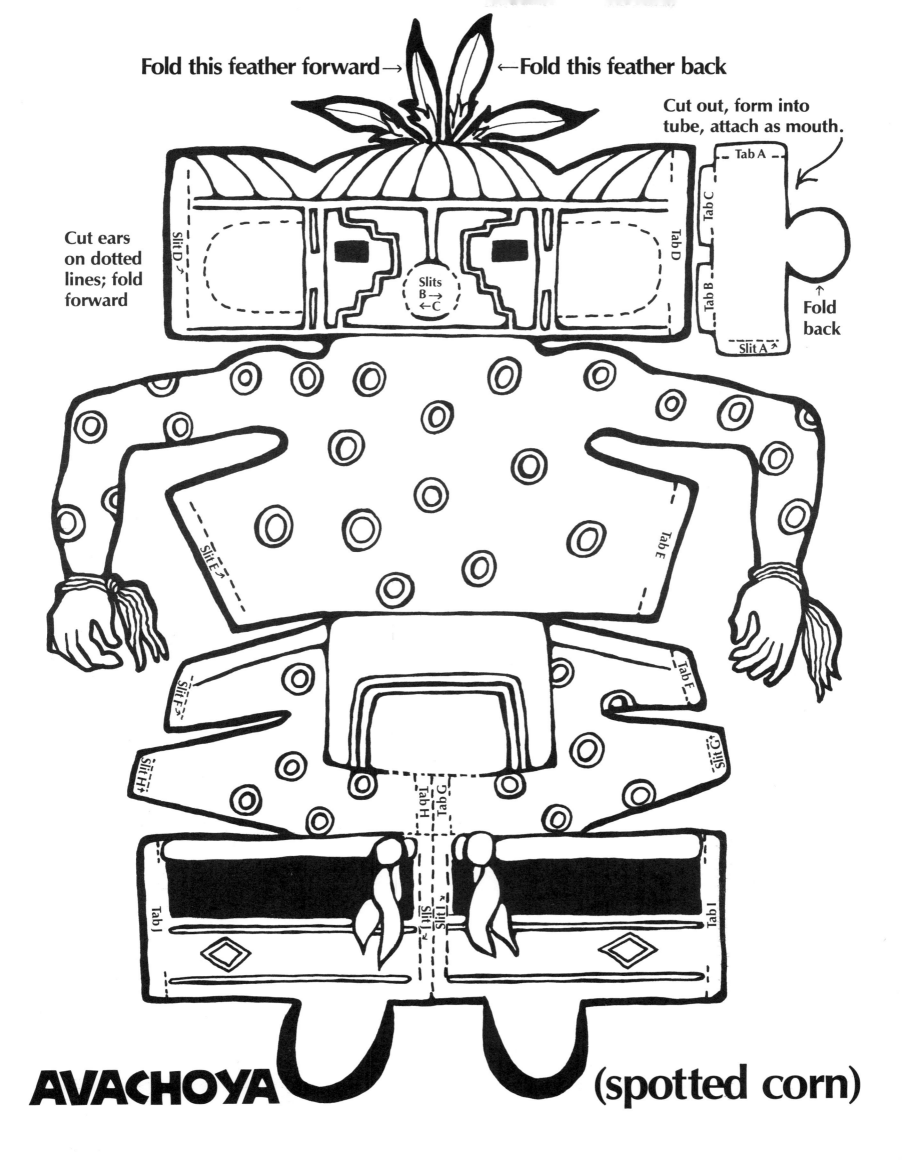

Fold this feather forward→   ←Fold this feather back

Cut out, form into tube, attach as mouth.

Tab A

Tab C

Cut ears on dotted lines; fold forward

Slit D

Tab D

Slits B→ ←C

Tab B

Slit A

Fold back

Slit E

Tab E

Slit F

Tab F

Slit H

Slit G

Tab H Tab G

Slit I

Tab J

Tab I

AVACHOYA (spotted corn)

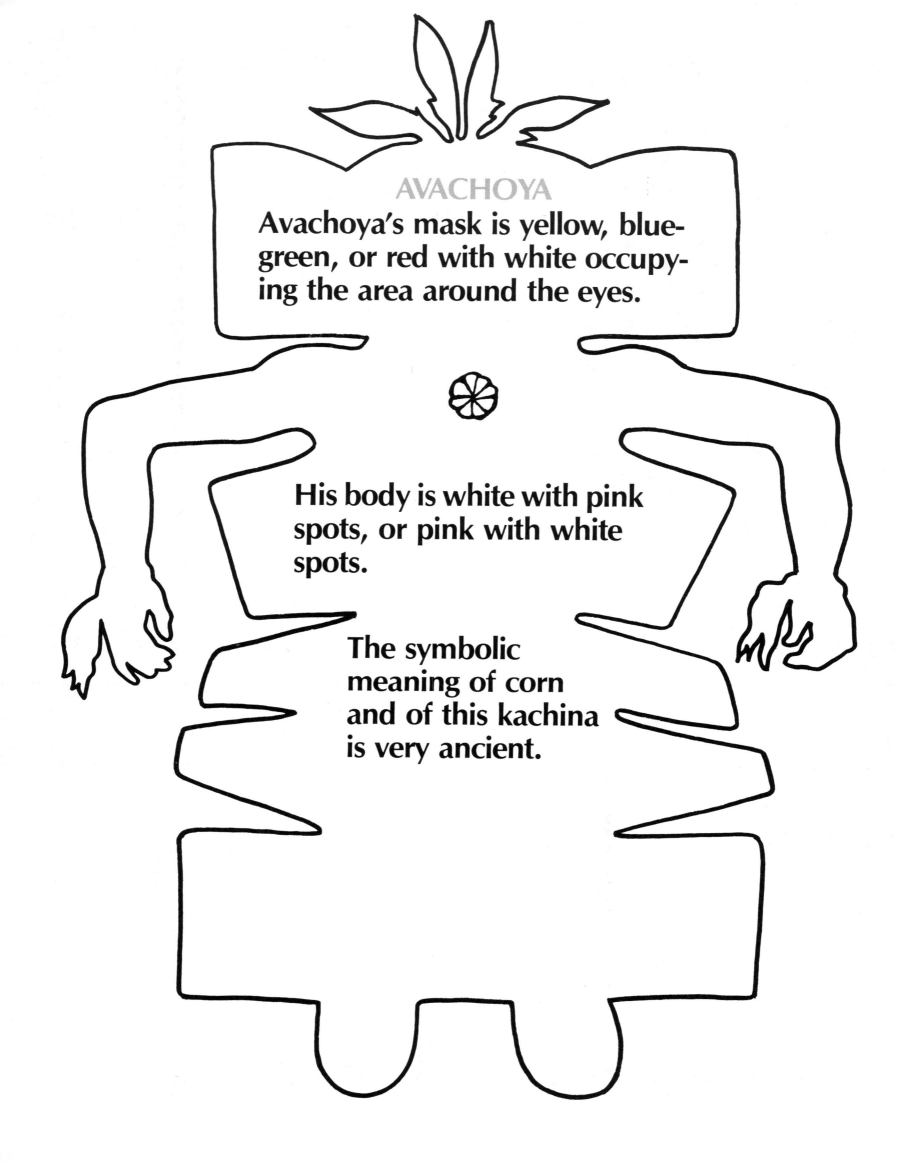

AVACHOYA

Avachoya's mask is yellow, blue-green, or red with white occupying the area around the eyes.

His body is white with pink spots, or pink with white spots.

The symbolic meaning of corn and of this kachina is very ancient.

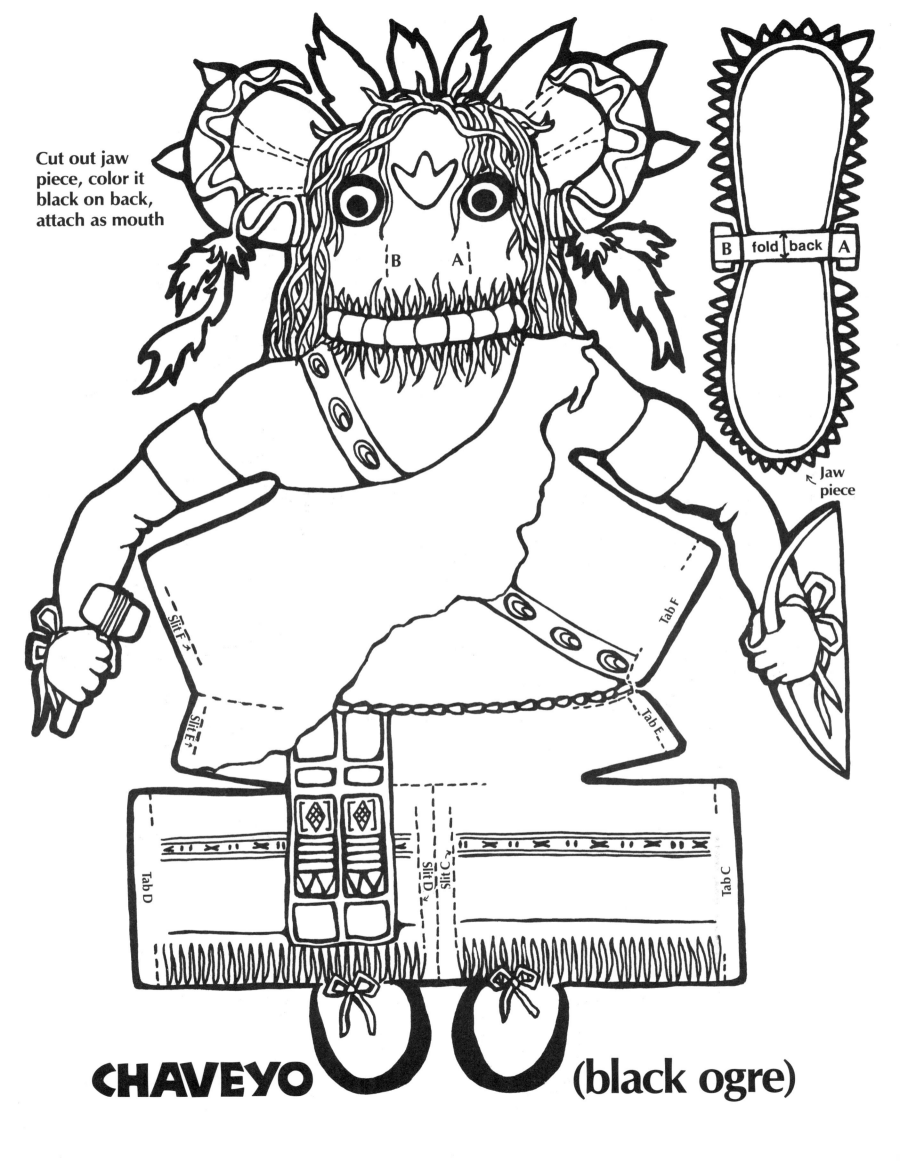

Cut out jaw
piece, color it
black on back,
attach as mouth

B   A

B   fold   back   A

Jaw
piece

Slit F

Slit E

Tab F

Tab E

Tab D

Slit D

Slit C

Tab C

CHAVEYO   (black ogre)

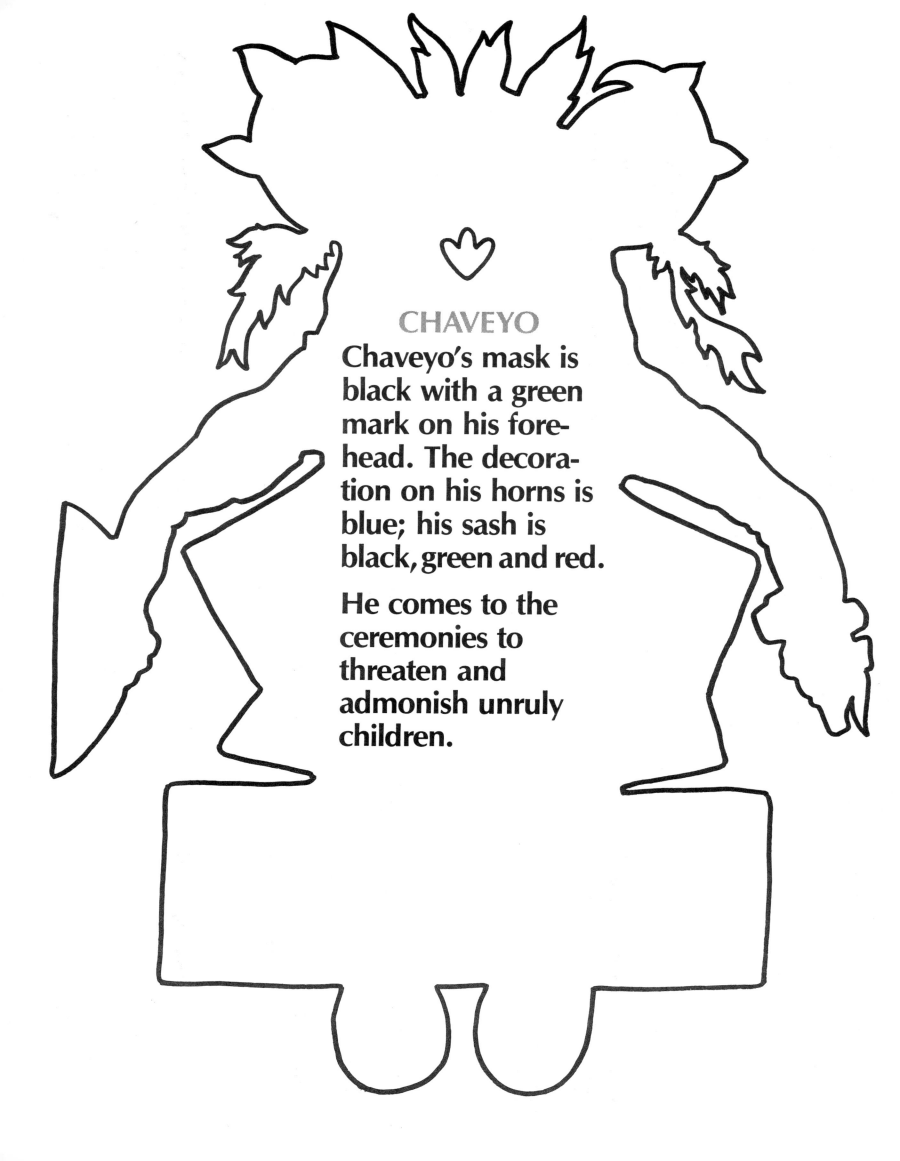

CHAVEYO

Chaveyo's mask is black with a green mark on his forehead. The decoration on his horns is blue; his sash is black, green and red.

He comes to the ceremonies to threaten and admonish unruly children.

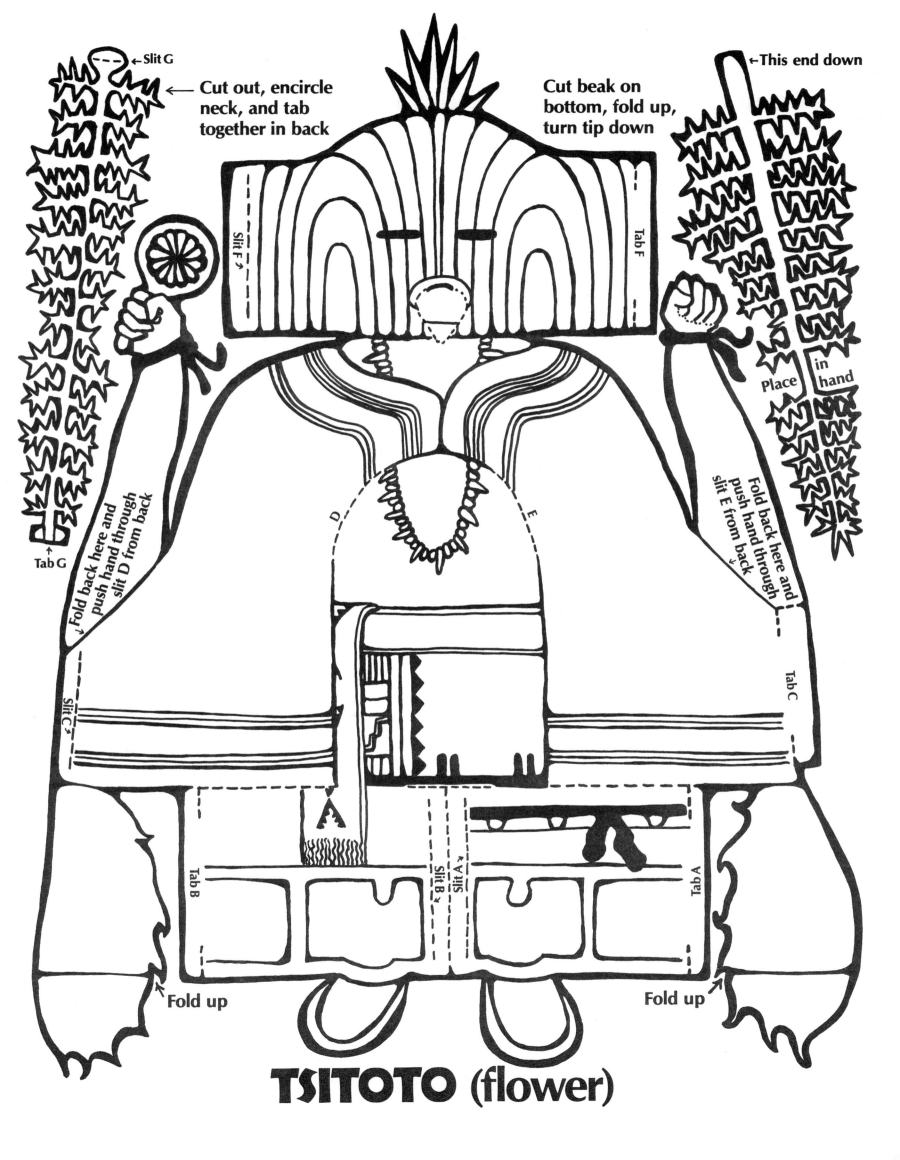

← Slit G

← Cut out, encircle neck, and tab together in back

Cut beak on bottom, fold up, turn tip down

← This end down

Slit F

Tab F

Place in hand

Fold back here and push hand through slit D from back

Fold back here and push hand through slit E from back

Tab G

D

E

Tab C

Slit C

Tab C

Tab B

A

Slit B

Slit A

Tab A

Fold up

Fold up

TSITOTO (flower)

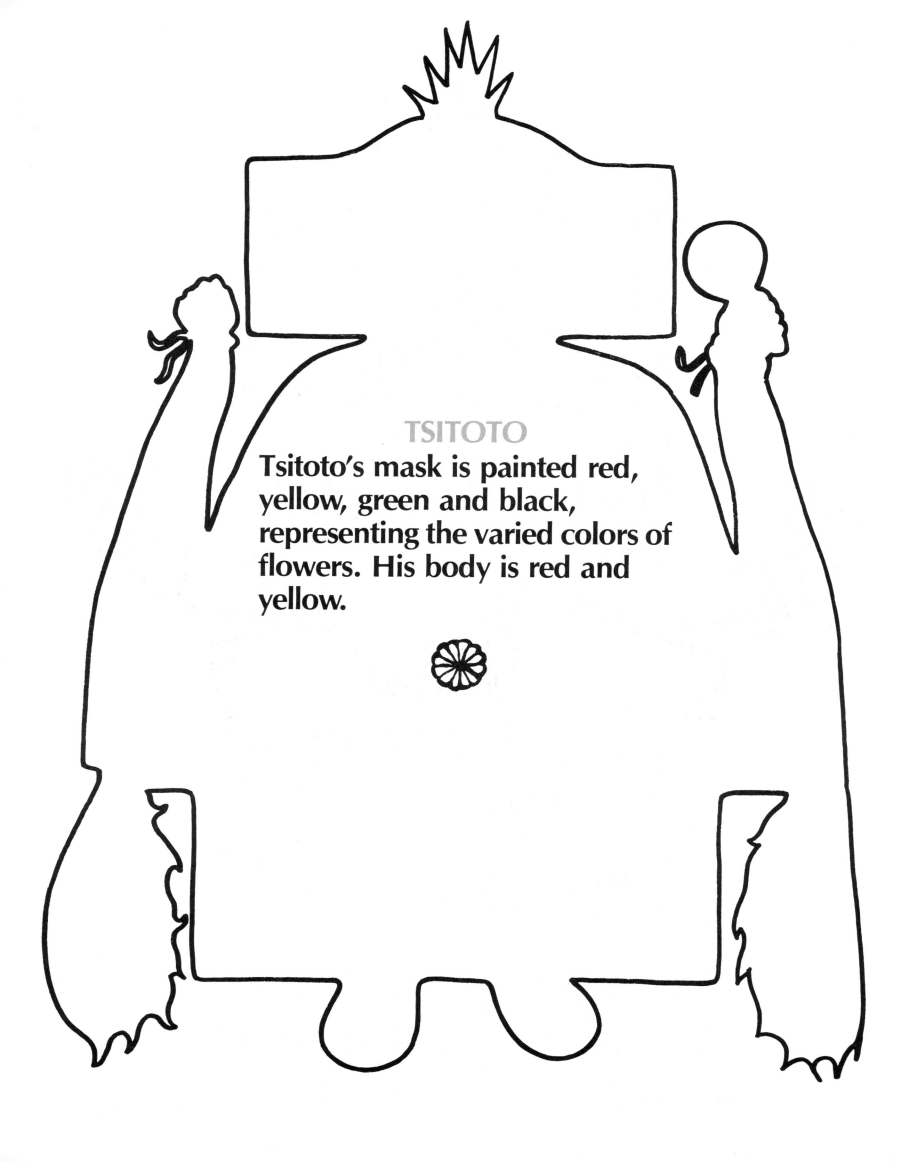

TSITOTO

Tsitoto's mask is painted red, yellow, green and black, representing the varied colors of flowers. His body is red and yellow.

HEMIS (homedance)

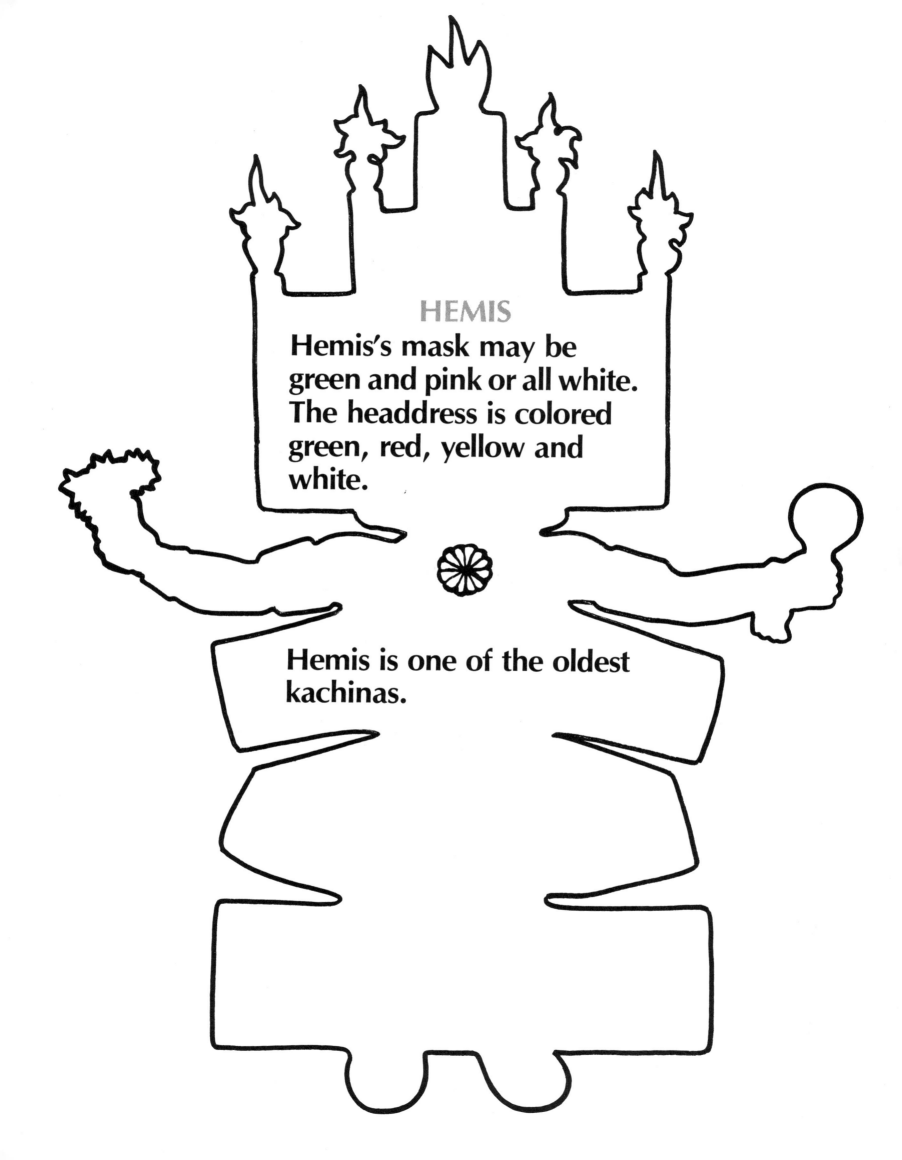

HEMIS

Hemis's mask may be green and pink or all white. The headdress is colored green, red, yellow and white.

Hemis is one of the oldest kachinas.

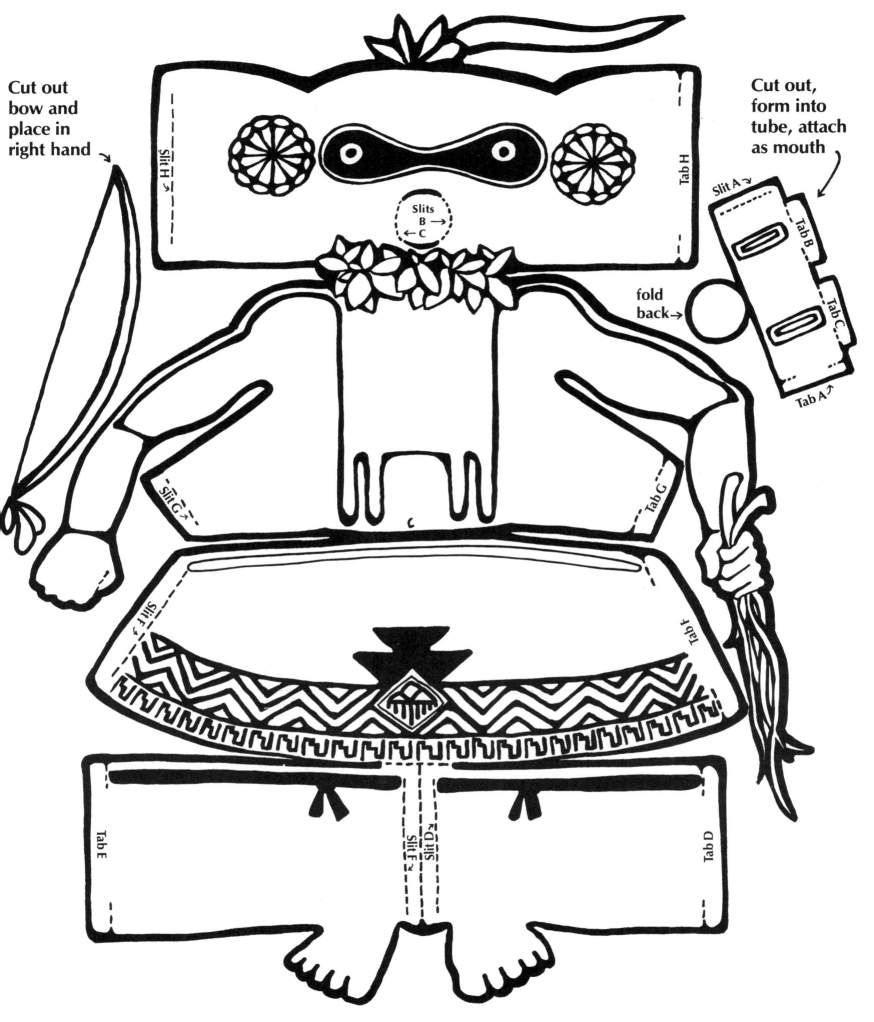

Cut out
bow and
place in
right hand

Cut out,
form into
tube, attach
as mouth

Slit H

Tab H

Slit A

Tab B

Tab C

Tab A

Slits
B
C

fold
back

Slit G

Tab G

Slit F

Tab F

Tab E

Slit F

Slit D

Tab D

SIP-IKNE (Zuñi warrior)

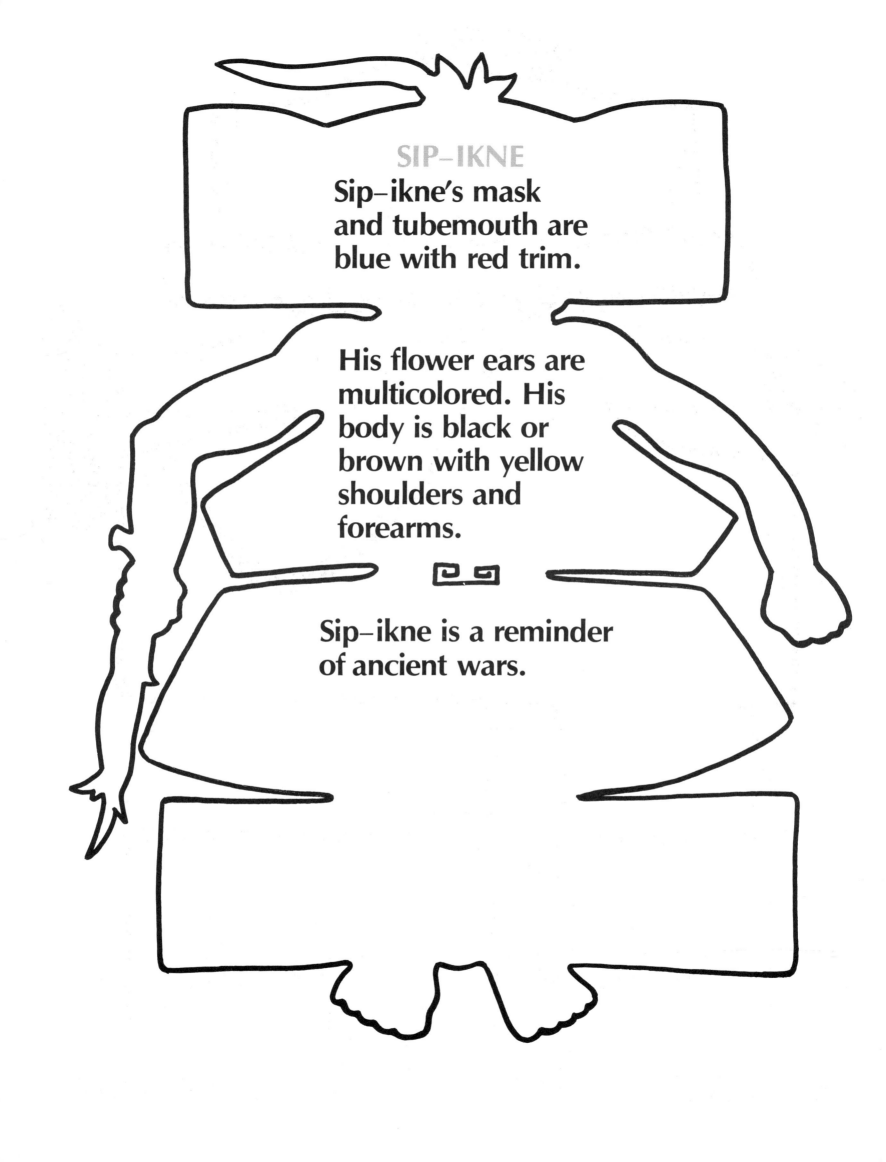

SIP–IKNE

Sip–ikne's mask
and tubemouth are
blue with red trim.

His flower ears are
multicolored. His
body is black or
brown with yellow
shoulders and
forearms.

Sip–ikne is a reminder
of ancient wars.

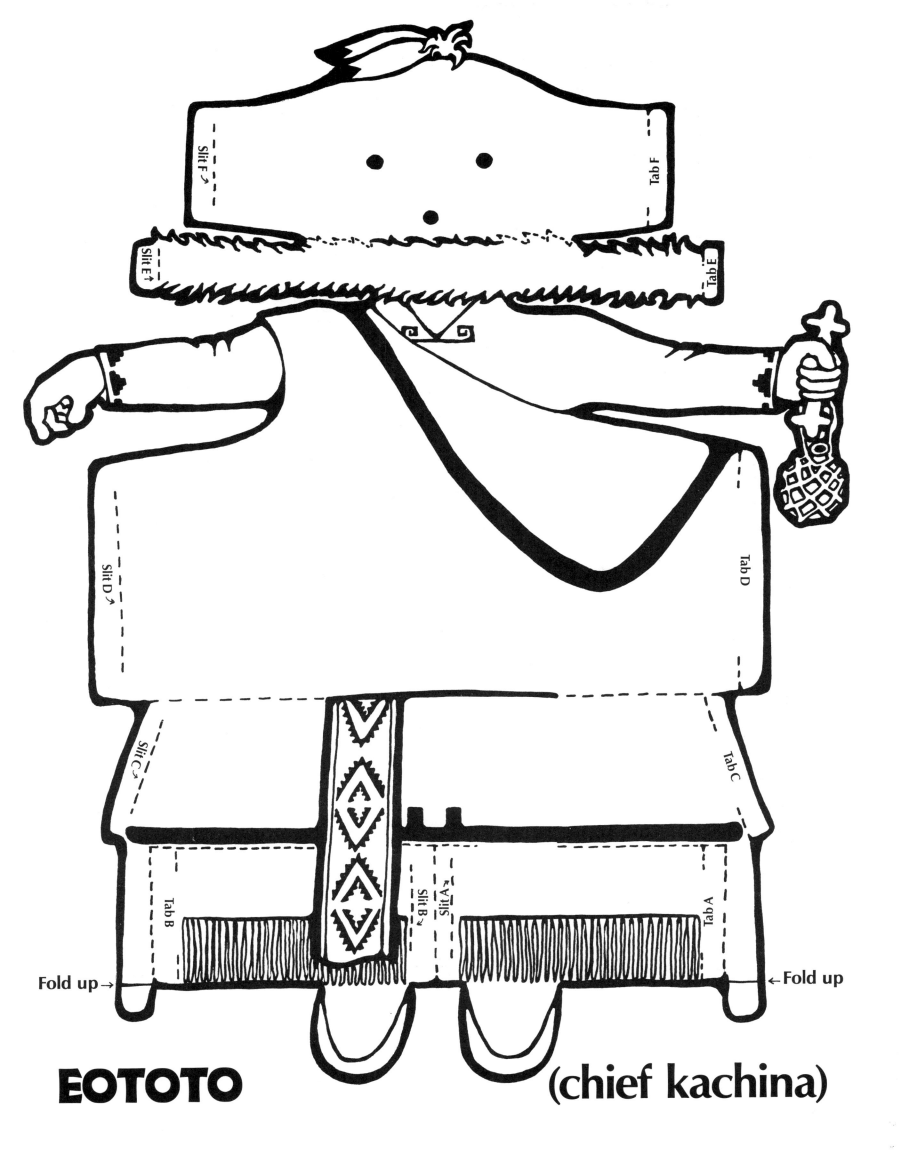

Slit F ↗

Tab F

Slit E ↑

Tab E

Slit D ↗

Tab D

Slit C ↘

Tab C

Tab B

Slit B ↘

Slit A ↘

Tab A

Fold up →

← Fold up

EOTOTO

(chief kachina)

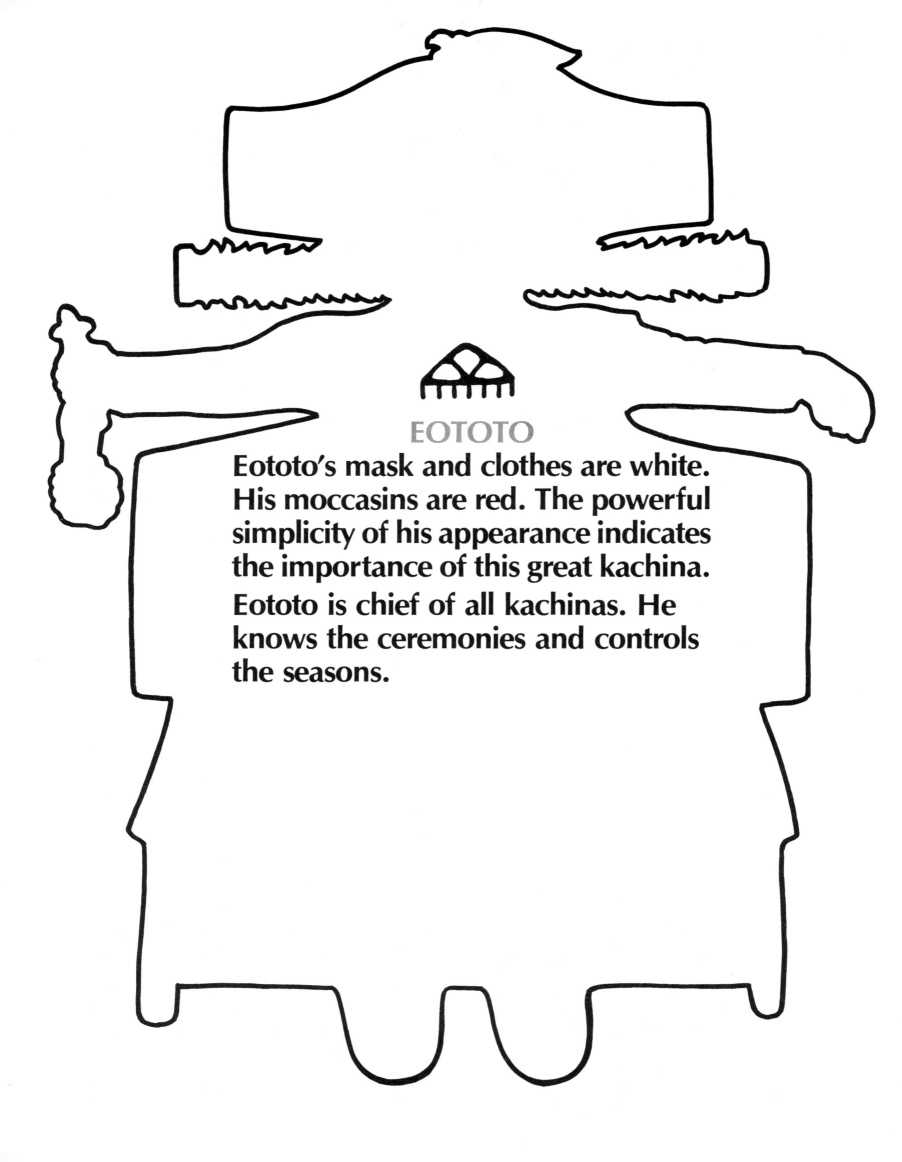

EOTOTO

Eototo's mask and clothes are white. His moccasins are red. The powerful simplicity of his appearance indicates the importance of this great kachina.

Eototo is chief of all kachinas. He knows the ceremonies and controls the seasons.

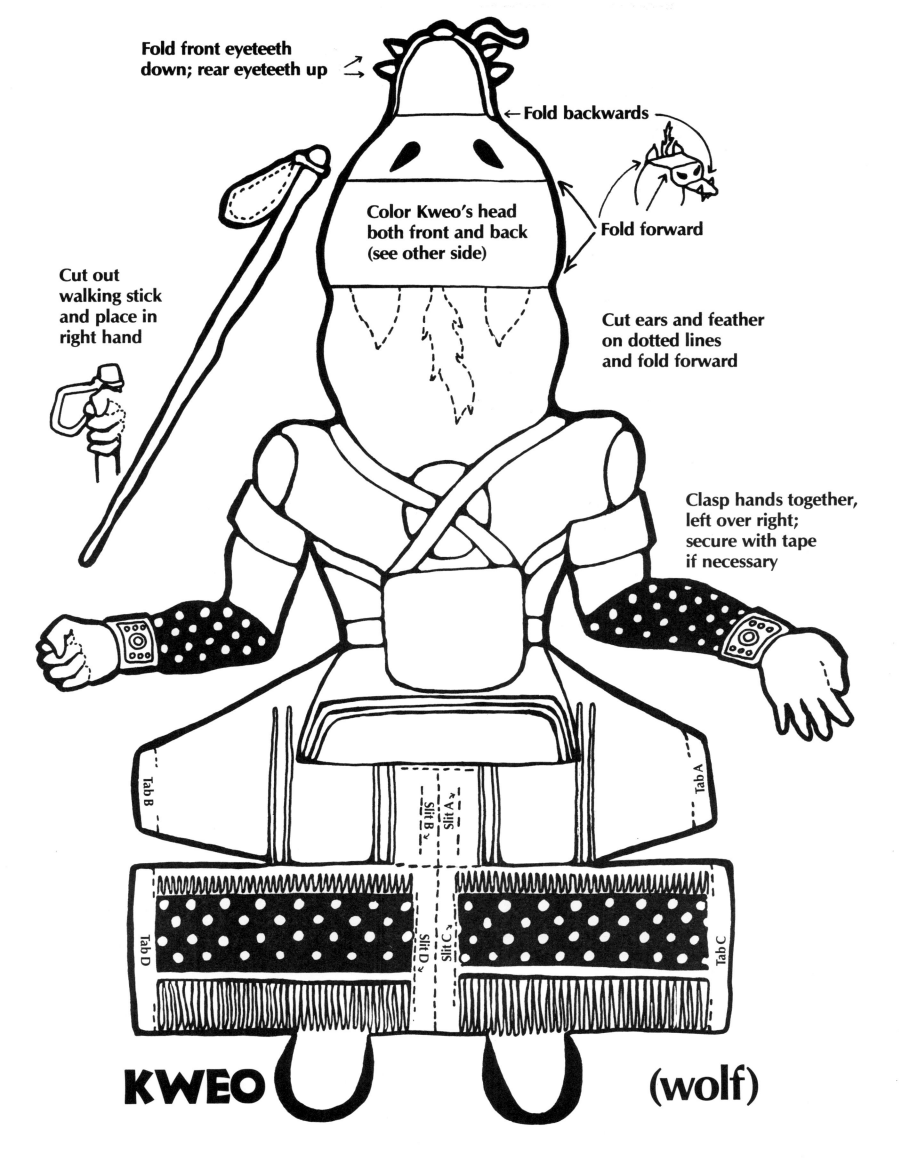

Fold front eyeteeth
down; rear eyeteeth up

← Fold backwards

Color Kweo's head
both front and back
(see other side)

Fold forward

Cut out
walking stick
and place in
right hand

Cut ears and feather
on dotted lines
and fold forward

Clasp hands together,
left over right;
secure with tape
if necessary

Tab B

Tab A

Slit A

Slit B

Tab D

Slit D

Slit C

Tab C

KWEO

(wolf)

KWEO

Kweo's mask and body are brown with white circles on his chest and shoulders. His armbands are blue.

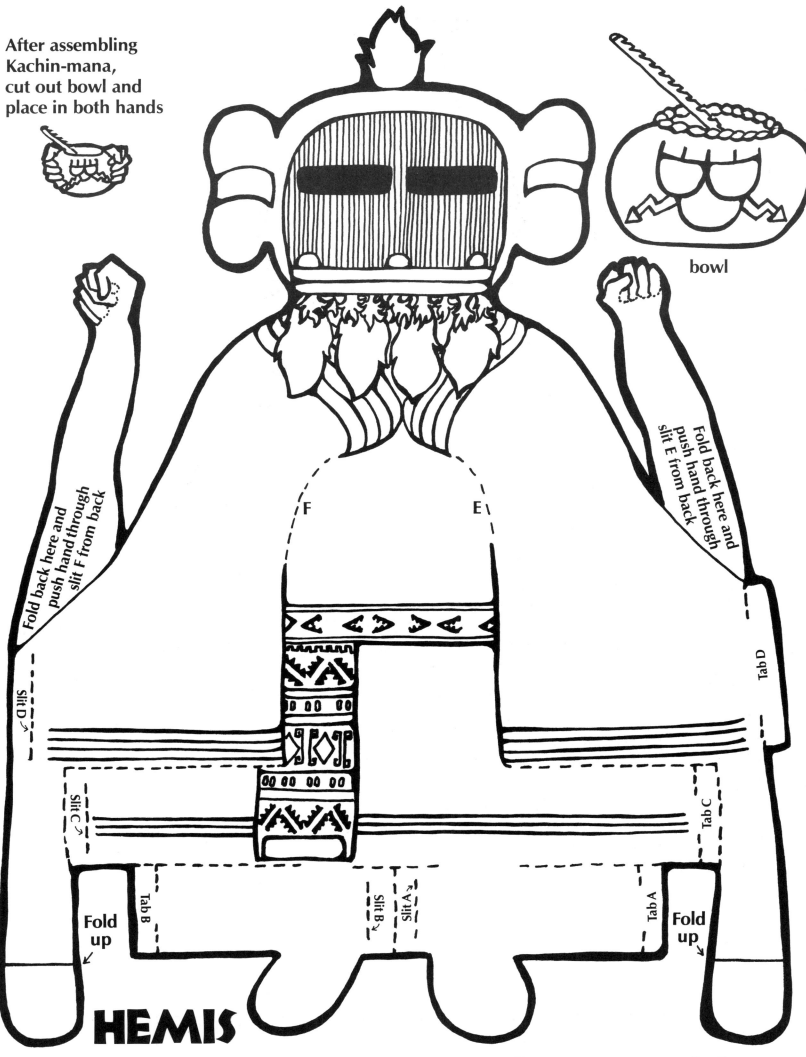

After assembling
Kachin-mana,
cut out bowl and
place in both hands

bowl

Fold back here and push hand through slit F from back

Fold back here and push hand through slit E from back

F

E

Slit D →

Tab D

Slit C →

Tab C

Tab B

Slit B →

Slit A →

Tab A

Fold up

Fold up

HEMIS
KACHIN-MANA (homedance maiden)

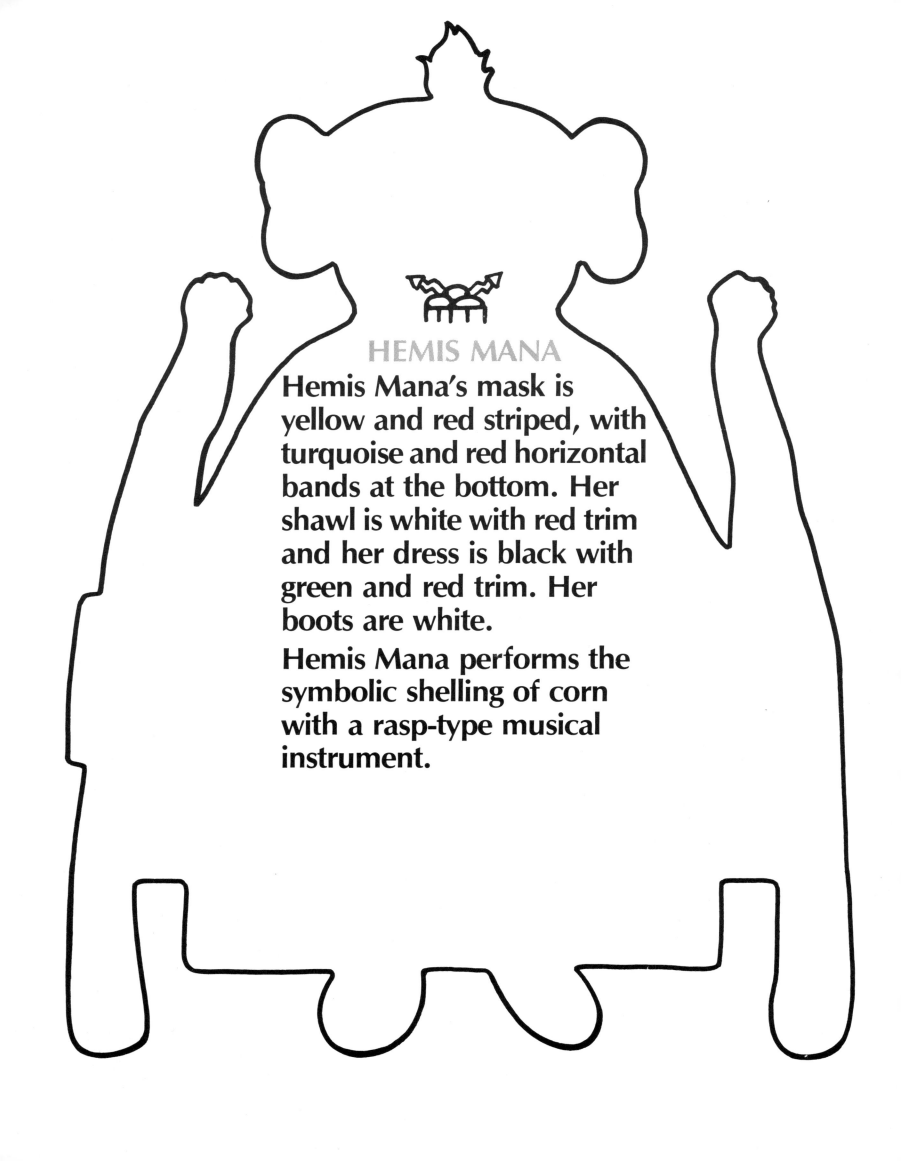

HEMIS MANA

Hemis Mana's mask is yellow and red striped, with turquoise and red horizontal bands at the bottom. Her shawl is white with red trim and her dress is black with green and red trim. Her boots are white.

Hemis Mana performs the symbolic shelling of corn with a rasp-type musical instrument.

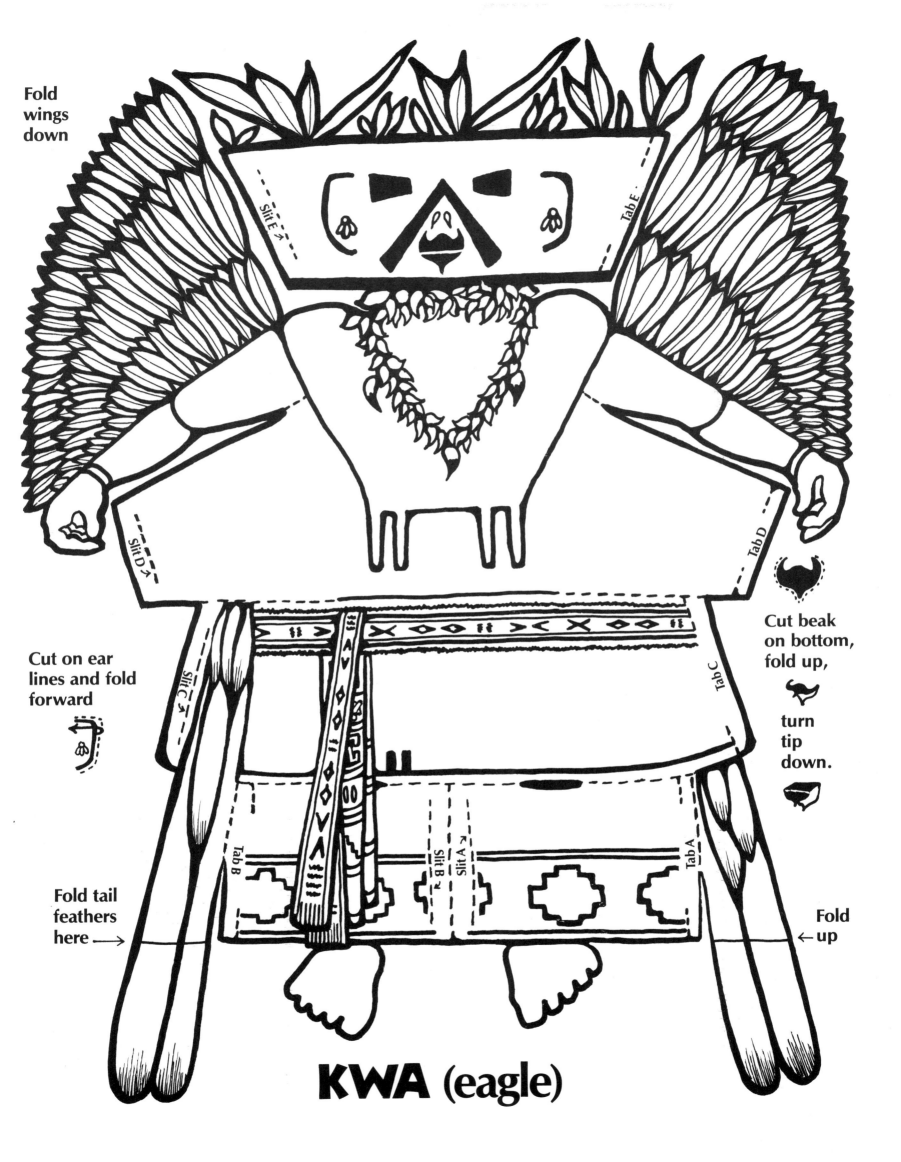

Fold wings down

Slit E

Tab E

Cut on ear lines and fold forward

Slit D

Tab D

Cut beak on bottom, fold up,

turn tip down.

Slit C

Tab C

Tab B

Slit B

Slit A

Tab A

Fold tail feathers here →

Fold up

KWA (eagle)

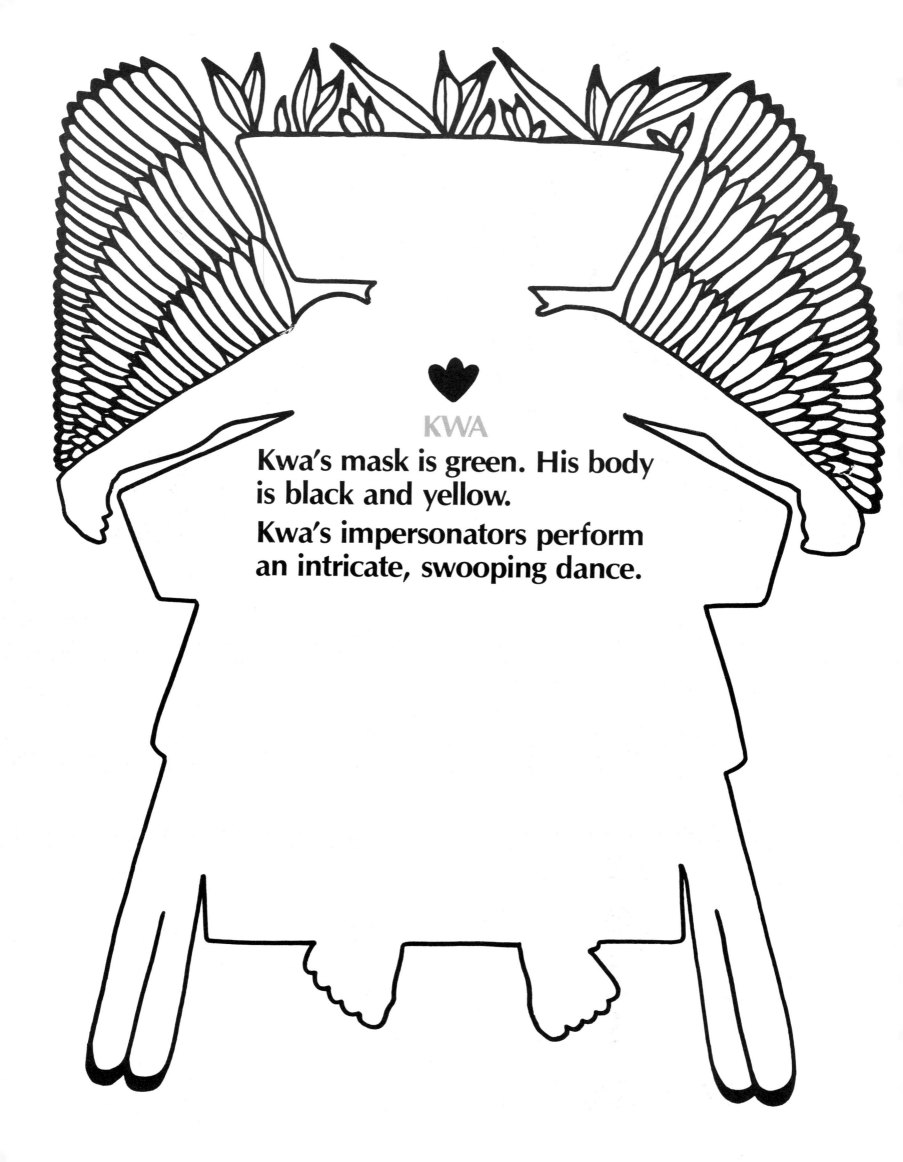

KWA

Kwa's mask is green. His body is black and yellow.

Kwa's impersonators perform an intricate, swooping dance.

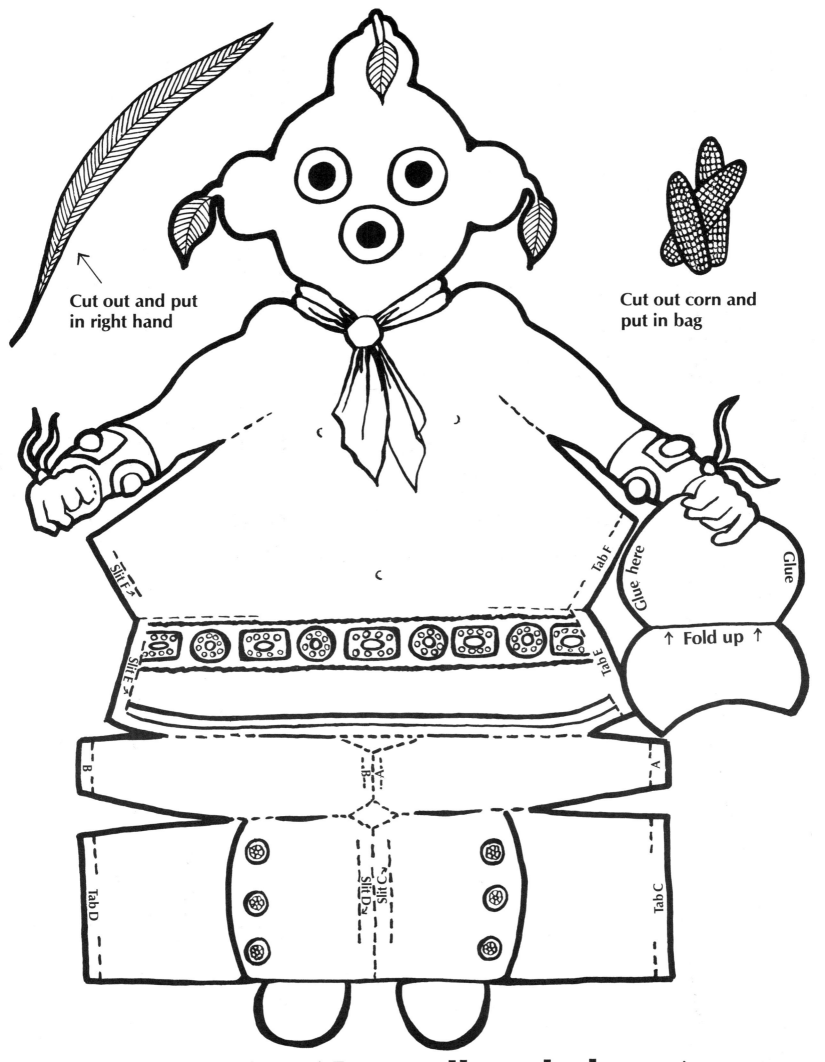

Cut out and put in right hand

Cut out corn and put in bag

Slit F

Tab F

Slit E

Tab E

Glue here

Glue

↑ Fold up ↑

B

B

A

A

Tab D

Slit D

Slit C

Tab C

KOYEMSI (mudhead clown)

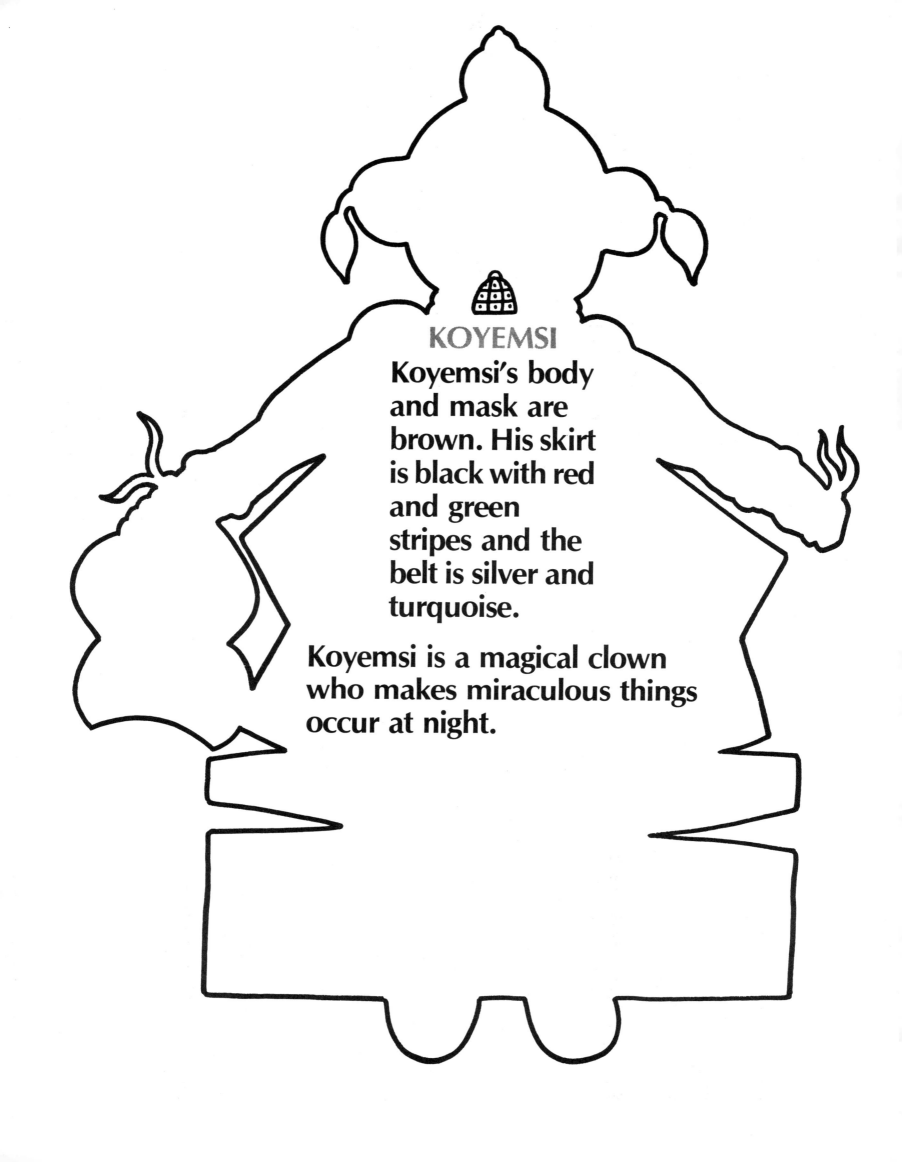

KOYEMSI

Koyemsi's body and mask are brown. His skirt is black with red and green stripes and the belt is silver and turquoise.

Koyemsi is a magical clown who makes miraculous things occur at night.

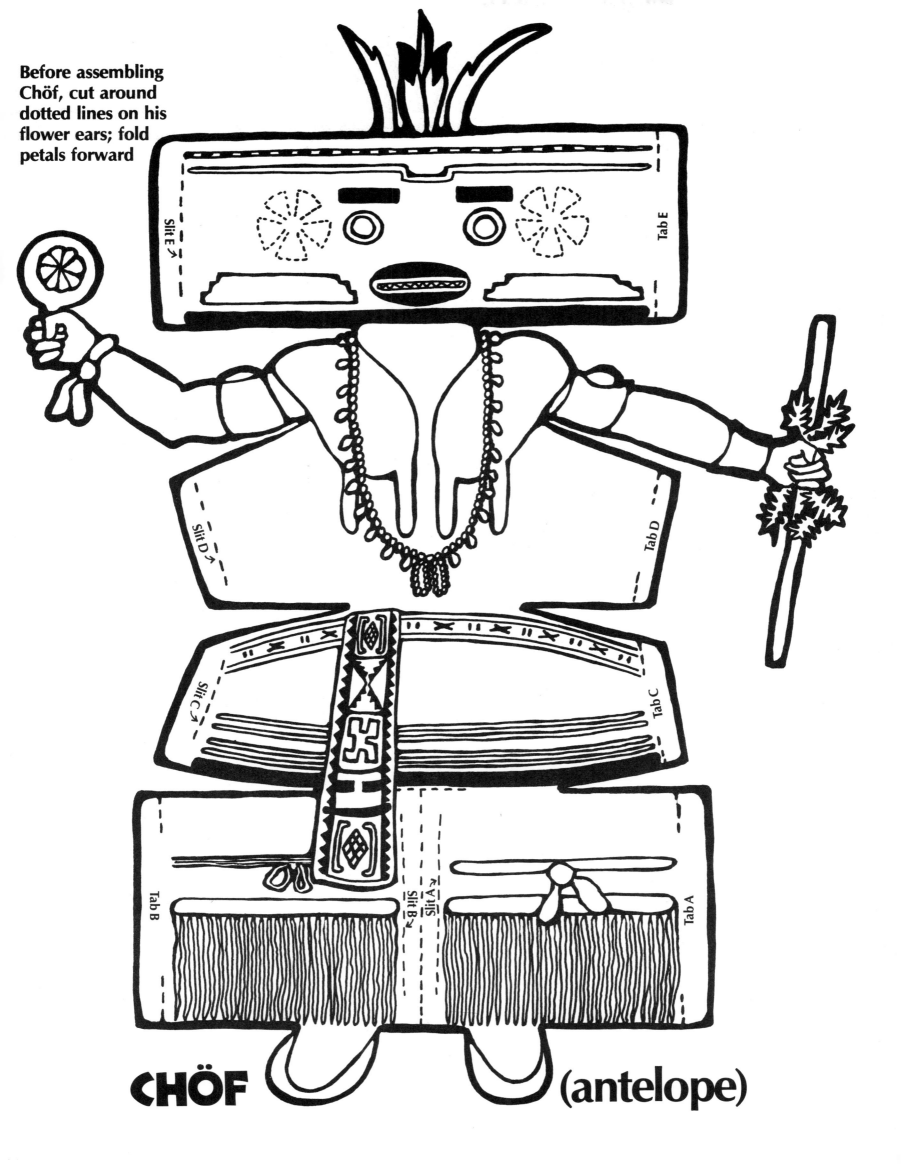

Before assembling Chöf, cut around dotted lines on his flower ears; fold petals forward

Slit E ↗

Tab E

Slit D ↗

Tab D

Slit C ↗

Tab C

Tab B

Slit B ↘

Slit A ↘

Tab A

CHÖF (antelope)

CHÖF

Chöf's mask may be rendered in various colors; blue, red and yellow are favored.

Chöf's flower ears symbolize his beneficial relationship to grass and flowers.

After assembling Tumas, cut out whip and place in right hand

whip

Fold back here and push hand through slit F from back

Fold back here and push hand through slit E from back

F

E

Slit D

Tab D

Slit C

Tab C

Tab B

Slit B

Slit A

Tab A

Fold up

Fold up

TUMAS OR
ANCWUSNASOMTAQA (crow mother)

TUMAS

Tumas's mask and moccasins are green. Her dress is black; her shawl is white with green, black and white designs.

Tumas is the mother of all kachinas.